By Chance or Choice

By

Donna Sako

Destiny is no matter of chance. It is a matter of choice. It is not a
thing to be waited for, it is a thing to be achieved.
- William Jennings Bryan

DEDICATION

The book is dedicated to my Book Club and Writer's Circle for their support and dedication and to all those who question their destiny and how to achieve it.

COPY WRITE & DISCLAIMER

This is a work of fiction. Names, characters, business, places, events, and incidents are either the products of the author's imagination or used in a fictitious manner. Any resemblance to actual person, living, or dead, or actual events is purely coincidental.

Table of Contents

Chapter 1: The Assignment

"Mark? Mark Antony?" Jules Carver, the editor of the magazine, was amid the meeting trying to awaken one of his writing staff. "M-A-R-K!" He yelled as he gave Mark a firm but polite shove as he paced behind Mark's chair.

Mark was dosing off once again during the meeting. He had a habit of doing so. Then slowly he opened one eye, yawned lifted his hands and began to rub his eyes. "Yes, Mr. Carver. Sorry I had a long night and apologize for dozing off."

"Mark you have a habit of dozing off. I do not know how you have time write when you sleep so much." Mr. Carver continued to walk around the large conference table eyeing all the staff. "We have a chance at interviewing the oldest living person on earth. Louise Antoinette Baker. She is turning 150 years old this year. She is a reclusive widow worth millions and lives hidden in the mountains of West Virginia. She rarely is seen. But scientists have studied her in the past and say she is remarkable. They, however, are sworn to silence about her. With her millions I am not surprised they hesitate to cross her. But I want someone to infiltrate her abode and do a story about her." Mr. Carver paused as he looked about the room. "Whomever I choose must be alert at all times, be able to penetrate her property, and gain her confidence. I want the story behind her life, who or what she is, and what hope she sees for mankind."

The room grew uncomfortably silent as Mr. Carver strolled behind those seated at the table. Everyone was acting rather shy. It seemed as if no one was elated to do the story. No one wanted to talk to a 150 year old. Every writer was under 50 years old except one—Mark Antony. He had just turned 50 on his last birthday.

"Mark Antony, you will do the story. Take as much time as you need but have it ready by the end of the year. Since it is March, you need to have it ready for our February issue."

Stunned by the words he heard, Mark wondered if his age is why he was chosen. Was this a signal that his days with the magazine were coming to an end? Mark nodded, "Will begin immediately, Sir. I guess I will be staying near her home for the next few months?"

"Yes, we have rented a lodging for you near her home."

As the meeting continued, Mark was in deep thought. Just how was he to gain access to her property? Could he get a job there? Landscaper? Could he make friends with the help she currently had? He had to do some research on her but little is really known. This might be his last story and he HAD to make it the best one he ever wrote.

Chapter 2: History

Mark had grown up in a small town in Maryland. He was married long ago to his high school sweetheart. But she died without bearing him any children 10 years after they were married. His job had sent him all over the world and, therefore, his life with his sweetheart, was not shared as most. His work made him a stranger to his wife and left him childless. Thus his work has been the only thing that keeps him alive. He has friends but they have family which to share their lives. But Mark, sadly, has lost his parents. He has no living relatives that he knows of. Mark is alone. Which is why the thought of losing his job or retiring is so frightening to him. Without his work he is lost.

"How does a 150 year old widow cope with loss?" thought Mark as he drove to his home to prepare for his journey. "She is a widow but did or does she have children? Are they alive?"

Pulling into his driveway, he began to ponder if a search engine would give him some clue to her relatives. As he entered his home, he removed his shoes at the door and walked into the kitchen lugging his briefcase. Things have not changed much since 2050 when he was born. But since Ms. Baker was born, technology improved a bit but lack of privacy, security, and safety had put a halt on much of it.

The 5G network was emitting signals that affected life on earth. It seemed to make it angrier and sicker. People and nature became violent. In 2030 due to its mass effects, mankind had to find a way to safely control electronic signals.

The environment was changed due to global warming. The melting of the ice caps created a slight change in the poles tilt. It seemed as if the earth was desperately trying to correct itself and recreate the balance that man helped to destroy. Man finally realized that choices and chance are similar. They both create change and can create an imbalance. The key is keeping balance.

It is now 2100. Over the last 150 years man has become more aware of his effects. But still man has not overcome his desire for power and greed. Those continue to need to be controlled.

As Mark contemplated the history that Ms. Baker would have experienced, he became more curious. This might be a really good story. She experienced quite a bit of history. The changes and adaptions she had to deal with and consider might make a good story.

After laying his briefcase on his kitchen table, he opened it to reveal his laptop. The outside looked much like what was created 100 years ago on the outside but smaller. Inside the programming was less cumbersome and could hold much more data. It also had the screen which projected and displayed the data, if requested, only via three dimension goggles for privacy. Otherwise, it would project an image seemingly in the air in front of him. He could move the information by moving his hands in either case by wearing a wrist band which allowed him to use the computer.

Mark did not feel like wearing his goggles, so he pushed a button with his left hand which was located on the band on his right wrist. The viewer appeared before him.

He paused, walked to his coffee maker to begin to brew his favorite drink. "I need to try and do some research here. That may give me a clue of how to begin." Carrying his full coffee cup to the table he began to do his search.

One interesting thing he found is, that when she was being studied, Louise was paid a hefty sum for her service. So she was able to use that income to invest and build her fortune. No record of living relatives were recorded. But that might be to preserve her privacy. So perhaps her local town could explain a bit of her history?

Feeling a bit disappointed, Mark closed his computer, finished his coffee and began to pack for his trip.

Chapter 3: The Trip

The next day Mark arose to very sunny day. The weather patterns have been returning to lower temperatures so the need for sun protection via protective clothing was no longer required. But since this was spring, he still needed a coat for warmth-just not a heavy one.

Dragging his suitcase on wheels to his car, he could not look directly into the sun but he did try to use his hand to give him some shade so he could see his path a bit clearer. As he placed his foot under his rear bumper, the trunk door rose allowing him to lift his suitcase into it. Besides his suitcase he had the usual emergency products for his safety.

As Mark entered his car using his thumbprint, his seat moved sideways which allowed him to sit and then it moved into place for driving. Seat belts were has been converted to automated force fields which automatically shield passengers. The car would not start unless they were activated.

Once Mark was ready to drive he just needed to give a verbal command. "Alexa, start engine." He had the choice to just enter the auto drive but due to the issues in the past and the fact he liked driving, he always chooses to drive himself. He likes being in control.

The GPS was active and began to verbally instruct. Off he went down the small city street to the beyond. Nature was still beautiful. It slowly was adapting to temperature changes but many species have died since 2020. New species developed. Nature is always evolving.

After 2 hours of driving and enjoying the scenery, he noticed his fuel needed recharged. He thought he had done so yesterday but perhaps not. Up ahead was a charging station off the highway. Mark turned toward the station. As he pulled to the charger he noticed that the sun dimmed and clouds were forming. A storm may be coming.

The charging station pumps weren't very busy but there were a few cars parked outside. He pulled up to one of the chargers, got out, and began to attach his car into the refuel plug after using his credit card. He would need probably 20 minutes to charge his car, so he chose to rush to the rest room.

Inside was the normal stuff: urinals, toilets, sinks, mirrors, garbage cans, hand air dryers. Not much improved over the last 100 years. Less water and paper were used. They keep trying to improve wiping afterward by using wet leaves specifically grown for that purpose. The government is pondering a law making everyone have their own toilet cloth. They would need to carry it with them to reduce using the trees. So the government, as usual, is fighting over shit.

"Done!" Mark announced as he was washing his hands. He leaned near the air dryer to finish. He made a quick glance in the mirror stroking his hair, turned and opened the door. His car was ready.

Once inside the car, he was once again on his way. The clouds were making things darker and slowly the rain began to fall. He turned on his wipers and slowed his speed since the rain was making it harder to see. He was only 30 minutes from his lodging according to Alexa GPS.

Suddenly a gust of wind came from nowhere. Mark was fighting for control but as he pulled right to stay on the road, the wind suddenly stopped which caused him lose control and take a plunge off the road and into a tree.

The motor stopped. Thankfully his force belt protected him from being projected out of the front window as well as shield him from the windshield glass which broke into pieces and flew in all directions.

The wind and rain continued along with lightning and thunder. Mark had passed out from the jolt of the crash.

A car pulled over alongside the wreckage. A hooded shadow left the car and made its way down the small hill toward Mark. Because of the fingerprint door lock, the shadow had to break the side door window to open the door and pull Mark from the vehicle. Soon police, ambulance, and firemen came.

The shadow retrieved Mark's baggage and computer placing them in their vehicle. Then, after giving information to the police, left the scene.

Still unresponsive, Mark was loaded on a gurney and taken by ambulance to the nearest hospital as his car was towed to the nearest garage.

Chapter 4: Awaking

Two doctors were reviewing X-rays from a monitor located on the wall inside the patient's room. Suddenly they heard a moan. "Mr. Anthony? Can you hear me?" The doctor said rather loudly as he rushed to his side.

Mark moaned and slowly peaked open one eye, then another. "Yes, I hear you. Please talk softer. I have a head ache."

"I am your attending physician, Dr. Walters, and this.." The doctor pointed to the man next to him. "..is Dr. Dye."

"How do you do Mr. Anthony?" Dr. Dye held out his hand hoping for a shake.

Mark gave him a puzzled look as he lifted his arm and shook his hand. "Where am I and how did I get here?"

"Apparently you crashed your car into a tree during one of our rain storms. The force of the crash and the effect of the pressure from the protective seat belt caused you to pass out. We have checked your health and did X-rays and you should be ready to leave soon."

"How is my car?"

"Well I heard it was heavily damaged and towed to the Max Garage. They are not far from here but you will need to call for transportation."

Mark was feeling rather exasperated. First he has to do a story on someone no one knows, then he had to drive over two hours, only to end in a hospital and now no transportation. "Where is my baggage, my computer?"

"We received nothing but you when you arrived. Perhaps they are still in your vehicle?" Dr. Walters responded. "Meantime, I will make a call to get you transportation. We have a volunteer who helps us occasionally in this situation. So no fee for it."

"I guess my wallet, ID's, charge cards, medical cards etc were on me?"

"Yes, that is how we knew your name, etc. Those things are here." Dr. Dye opened the drawer on the stand next to the bed.

"Thank you so very much." The doctors finished filling in the forms on the bed and then left the room. A nurse came in as they left. "Mr. Anthony?" Mark nodded. "I have received your exit papers. Your clothes are in the closet" She pointed to a door across the room. "I will take these." Picking up the papers on the bed she smiled. "Relax. All is okay. Once you are dressed please exit the room and turn right. Down the hall on the left is the discharge station."

As the nurse left the room, Mark slowly sat up feeling a bit dizzy. Once that was over, he placed his feet on the floor and made his way to the closet. He was happy all his clothes, including his shoes were there and began to dress. Once dressed he emptied the drawer containing his wallet and slowly made his way down the hall still feeling a bit groggy. On the left, as instructed, was the discharge station. "Hello. I am Mark Anthony and I am here to get discharged. Also I believe transportation has been arranged for me. A volunteer?"

"Yes. Anna will be here shortly. Meantime please sign these papers concerning your medical insurance and your release."

After Mark completed the tasks he moved to a chair in the waiting room. There was a TV activated and news cast was reporting on the prior day's weather storm. Apparently, the storm was a rare happening and caused damage. He felt rather lucky he lived through it.

About ten minutes later, Anna reported to the discharge desk for her assignment. After a short conversation, she entered the waiting room looking for Mark.

Mark was alone in the room. "I am guessing you are Mark Anthony?" Anna asked as she waved.

"Yes, I am." Mark was a bit surprised that Anna, a woman, would be driving him. Most women were afraid of being mugged and thus did not do professional driving. He rose from his chair and offered his hand in greeting.

Anna shook his hand, "Where would you like to go?"

As he looked into her eyes he felt that question was a bit awkward. You see he was a bit attracted to her. But he stopped himself from saying what he really wanted to say, "I have to go to Max Garage to check on my vehicle. I was in a crash yesterday during the storm and, depending on my car's situation, I may need transportation to my lodging."

Smiling Anna nodded, "I know them well. Follow me." With that they walked slowly down the adjoining hallway toward the exit.

Chapter 5: The Auto

"So how long have you been driving professionally?" Mark asked.

Anne laughed, "I don't drive professionally. I do it as a favor to the hospital when they need me."

"So you donate your time?"

"Yes, they have been very helpful to me in the past and this is one of the ways I repay them."

They reached the Anna's car. Using her thumbprint she open the driver's seat. "Open driver's side door." Then looking at Mark, "You can get in now." Mark went to the other side of the vehicle and entered. He watched as Anna prepared for the journey. The order "Buckle up." Was given and the engine started.

"So what brings you to our small town, Mark?"

How do I answer that? Thought Mark. He really did not want to give his purpose away but he really never came up with a story yet. "I am kind of a traveler." Well at least that wasn't a lie. He thought. "I'm renting a lodging locally and looking for, perhaps, landscaping work?" That was not a lie either. He thought that might be an opening for the Baker property.

Anna gave him big smile. "How much landscaping have you done?"

Oops! Now, does he lie or tell the truth? What a dilemma! He really does not want to lie but he never did landscaping in his life. He was always a writer! "Well, Anna, truth be known, I am a writer and want to do a story which may include landscaping." Mark's brain was working. "Whew! Not a lie. This is harder than I thought. "

"I might be able to help you. Where is your lodging?"

Now he had to remember the address. "I believe it is called Destiny Calls Campground? I have cabin 2."

"Know it well. After we check on your car I will take you there."

Ahead on the left was Max Garage. Anna pulled into the parking lot and parked. There was a large metallic building off to the side of the smaller office one. Anna locked the car, after which they exited and began walking toward the office door. A large OPEN sign was in the window. As they entered, Mark was anxious.

"Good morning! How may I help you?" Max, the owner, greeted them. Max was about 6 feet tall and very muscular.

"I believe you have my vehicle. I was in that rain storm last night and hit a tree."

"Oh, yes. So sorry, man. The car is totaled. The engine block was hit hard and it would cost too much to replace it."

Mark's jaw dropped. "So what do I do now?"

"Well, it depends on you. Do you want a new or used vehicle? Or do you want to rent?"

Mark was thinking about his budget. Ouch! He never prepared for replacement of either until a few years from now. "I can't afford a new car. Where can I get a used one?"

"I don't sell cars but Anna can take you to a local dealer. Meantime, what do you want us to do with the car? I would be willing to buy it, as is, for say….300 dollars."

Exasperated once again. He was happy he owned it outright but a bit overwhelmed that it was now only worth 300 dollars. With a long sign Mark replied, "Okay, deal. But I am missing my luggage and computer and other items. I want to get them back before the sale."

Max walked Mark to the car and gathered all his emergency stuff, emptied his glove compartment and other areas but could not find his computer or luggage. "Max, where is my luggage and computer?" Mark asked now in a panic.

"I never saw them. Have you checked with the police? Sometimes they gather those things for you—especially if the car is severely damaged like yours."

Anna could see the anguish that Mark was going through. "Mark, let's check out your lodging first. Perhaps someone took them there?"

"Who and how would they know where to take it?

"Where there any identification papers with the luggage or in your wallet?"

"The hospital had my wallet. It did have the address where I was going in it. Could they have given it to the police?"

"Perhaps, yes." Anna watched as Mark was getting restless. "You want to go the lodge or to the police first?"

"Let's go to the police, please."

So off they went. Mark's frustration was getting worse and Anna was bit worried for him. "Mark, calm down. The police will help."

Once they reached the station Mark was quick to rush out the car door leaving Anna in the dust. He almost flew through the door. Upon seeing the main desk, he sped to the policemen who was manning it. "Officer, I was in a collision yesterday, my car was totaled, and my luggage and computer are missing. Can you help me?"

Noticing Mark's fear and worry, the officer spoke, "I am sorry for what you have gone through. What is your name so I can find any records we might have?"

"Mark Anthony."

"You ran into a tree?" The officer was looking in his computer.

"Yes, do you have my stuff?"

"Sorry, no we don't…"

"Where is it? Can you help me?"

"Mr. Anthony, please let me finish." The officer said with an impassioned plea. "Your things were taken by the person who found you after the crash and called us. We told them of your lodging from your wallet information. They said they worked at the park and would drop the stuff off to your lodge."

"What was their name? And contact number?" Mark asked.

"Strange, I don't have that." The officer was quite perplexed.

"Okay, I will deal with that later if my stuff is not there!" Mark was angry that they had no name on file.

Anna stood there a bit stunned by Mark's actions. "Mark, calm down. It will be alright I'm sure." Mark ran out the door and stood waiting for Anna at the car.

"Hurry, Anna, I need to make sure my things are there."

As Anna and Mark entered the car, their conversation stopped. Anna was feeling sad and worried; Mark was feeling frustrated and angry. He was so into himself he did not realize how much his actions affected Anna.

Chapter 6: The Lodge

As they drove along, both sides of the road were hidden in forest. Only a few vehicles were being seen. The road began to climb up a mountain filled with turns and dips but always heading up. The sun occasionally peaked through the open areas of the trees. Wild flowers also edged the road below. Soon, just ahead, was a sign along the road "Destiny Calls Campground". "I believe your lodge is down this main drive." Anna said as she made a right turn into the campground. "You said your cabin is 2? Right?"

Mark nodded, "Yes, 2." On the right side of the road was number 1, on the left side 2. Anna pulled into the driveway and parked her car. "Thank you, Anna. I am so sorry I have been a pain. It is just that so much has happen to me in the last few days and I feel it is overwhelming."

They left the car and walked to the front door.

"I'm glad I could help. Now let's check out the cabin. Do you have your key?"

"Key? What key? No one gave me a key." Panic was setting in once again.

"Mark, you wait here. I will go to the main office, explain the issue and return with the key." Before Mark could respond, Anna was inside her car and drove away. All the wrong things that have happened were starting to feel like a sick joke. To fill in the time, Mark began to try and peek inside the windows. He then walked around to the back of the cabin. Suddenly he was amazed at the view. There was a rear deck which not only gave him the view of the forest but also, due to the slope of the hill in the rear, gave him a lofty view of the lake that the cabins surrounded.

He made his way back to the front and found Anna waiting for him. "I was beginning to worry that you walked off."

"No. Anna, I was admiring the view."

"Here is your key." He took the key from her hand and could feel the soft touch of her fingers.

"Thanks!" Mark opened the door and Anna followed him in. The room was quaint and warm. There was a fireplace mid room on one of the walls. A hallway was on the left of the fireplace and another on the right. They walked to the one on the left and found a restroom and two bedrooms. "Hallelujah!" Mark yelled as he danced with glee. "My baggage and computer ARE here!"

Anna was laughing as Mark filled up with joy. "I told you. They would be here."

"Yes, you did. I guess I need to listen to you more."

"Well I have to leave, now. But I will check in with you tomorrow and we can hunt for you replacement car. Say 10 AM? "

"Great! See you then!" After she left, he was a little sad that she had to go but he had already took up so much of her time today. He went down the other hallway and found the kitchen which led to the deck. Opening the drapes, he could see that wonderful view. "I wonder if there is any food." He opened the refrigerator and to his surprise—there was! Milk, eggs, bread, butter, some lunch meat. In the freezer above there were some frozen vegetables, fruit, meat, and PIZZA!

He glanced at the stove and also noticed pots and pans hanging from the ceiling. There was a drawer with some silverware and cooking utensils, knives. Everything he needed to live here was provided. His boss must have arranged it.

By now, the pizza was sounding very yummy so his unpacked it, turned on the oven, and began to make his dinner. He was starving.

Once his dinner was ready he gathered a plate and began to eat his pizza while sitting on the deck. This job is almost like a vacation: except for the collision, his temporary loss of his luggage and computer, his passing out and stress, loss of his car, and not having keys. But then there was getting his keys and meeting Anna. So the day kind of balanced out. Among the negative things that happened, good things did as well.

Chapter 7: Finding New Transportation

As 10 AM was coming close, Mark was finishing up the dishes from the pizza and breakfast. He was looking forward to seeing Anna and looking for his new car.

There was a knock at the door. Mark gave himself a quick look at his reflection in the glass of the window, stroked his hair and with a broad grin opened the door. But instead of Anna his was looking at Max from the garage along with a huge truck parked in his driveway.

"Hello, Max, what are you doing here?"

"Well, Anna called me and ask me to take you around to look for a car. She had other things to do and knows I know about cars and felt I would be better to help you find an appropriate used car. I owe her, so I am here to help."

Quite a bit disappointed Mark forced a grin. "Great!"

Locking his door, making sure he had his wallet, Mark then followed Max to his truck. As Max did the normal commands to open doors and get the vehicle started, Mark was busy wondering what Anna's other things might be.

"Okay Mark. What kind of vehicle do you want? Another car like before or something different?"

He pondered for a moment, "Well Max, I really liked my other car. So something similar is what I probably would like."

"I know a dealer we can check out." Max smiled and progressed driving with confidence. "Now the dealer I've got in mind is a relative. He can be a bit overwhelming but let me help you get a good deal."

Mark was not so sure the "relative" was a good idea. They might be cahoots and trying to scam him. So he planned to be very wary.

Soon they pulled into a rather large dealership apply named Fox's Den. The name, even more, made Mark nervous. He was literally entering the fox's den. Could this assignment get any weirder? It seemed so much is going wrong. The amount of stress from these few days just seems to keep building.

"Here we are!" cheered Max as he pulled to a stop inside the parking lot. "I can't wait for you to meet my cousin Sly!"

Okay, Fox's Den was one thing, but now cousin Sly? "You're kidding right?" Asked Mark. "His name is Sly Fox?" The look of horror was upon his face.

Max grinned from ear to ear, "Yep! His parents had a real sense of humor! Sly is short for Sylvester. At least that is what they say." He gave Mark a wink.

In horror, Mark left the truck and followed Max through the maze of used cars. "See anything that strikes your fancy?" Mark tried to ignore Max as he began to fixate on the variety of vehicles available. Especially when Max would leap for joy and point to some car screaming "How about this one! Or that one!"

"Pointless" thought Mark as rambled about. "How can I trust this guy? Let alone, any Sly Fox?"

Then as he tripped over a crack in the asphalt, he fell right into was his dream car. Falling head over heels in love with it on first sight. But he could not give away how much he loved it and wanted it. That would just play into the Sly Fox.

Max watched as Mark gently touched the outside of vehicle. Mark seemed to caress every inch with dove like wooing. He then touched the handle to open the door. Nothing. It would not open.

"I could get Sly to let you drive it." Max smiled but hesitated. "If you like?"

Nodding, Mark, turn toward Max, "Yes, I think I would like that." He felt he just gave away any hope of a good deal.

Max ran into the dealership and quickly returned with a man who was just as tall and muscular as Max. Only he wore a suit and had a well-trimmed beard. He had the same wide grin as Max and offered his hand as he approached. "Hello! Welcome to Fox's Den! I am Sly, Max's cousin." Mark shook his hand but was still leery. "I understand you had your vehicle totaled during the storm 2 days ago. Sorry about that man. But I can probably put you back on your "feet" so they say."

"He is trying to schmooze me" thought Mark as he once again forced a friendly grin.

"Max tells me you are interested in driving this beauty." Sly, as the Fox he was, he opened the car door for Mark.

Now Mark was getting very anxious once again but this time in a good way. He was excited that he could actually be sitting and driving his dream car. Now I know most people their dream car is a race car or some high priced sports or ritzy high fashion car. But to Mark, this small station wagon was his dream. It brought back memories of picnics, amusement parks, ball games, family trips, and fun times with friends and family. Yes, it was a rather old used car but the memories it held for him far outweighed any lust for the newer, fancier ones.

"Yes, I would like a test drive."

They all entered the wagon and Max drove throughout the city and country for about thirty to forty-five minutes. Casual conversation occurred but Mark was busy mostly with pondering the price and how much he loved it.

Once back to the dealership they entered and made their way to the deal room, or as Mark saw it, the Fox's den. They all sat down and began to hustle.

"Now I know you're thinking that Max here," Sly motioned to Max, "is my cousin so you think he will choose me over you when it comes to negotiation. Right?" Mark shyly nodded. "But what you need to know is Max is going to check out the wagon. Then, if it meets safety and is in the good shape I know it is, I will make you an offer." With that Max left the room and strolled down to the mechanics room. "So while he is a doing that, Help yourself to the refreshments behind you and here is the remote for the TV. Make yourself at home. Feel free to use the couch or magazines as well. I have other things to do and will be back when Max is finished." With that Sly left the room.

Fortunately, the walls inside the dealership were made of glass and he could see both Max checking the car and Sly entering his office to talk to another person who was waiting for him. This made him feel a little more comfortable.

Mark went to the refreshment table got some coffee and a donut and sat on the couch. He could still see Max and Sly and take some time to relax.

While he was watching them, he saw Sly get a phone call. He seemed both happy and nervous during the call. Max was busy checking the brakes, the engine, and other parts on the wagon. He even checked the tires and windshield wipers. Max was, indeed, giving it the full inspection.

Once finished, Max made his way back to Mark. He did not talk to anyone else before him.

Max entered and spoke, "Mark, I did a full inspection and the wagon is in remarkably good condition. I would not pay any more than $10,000 for it though since it is still a rather old car."

"Thank you Max. I am not sure if you knew it, but I could see all the work you did. For that I am truly grateful."

"No problem. Now we need to try and get it for less than that."

A few minutes later Sly Fox returned to the room and sat in his usual negotiating chair. "Well, Max, how did she do?"

"Sly, the wagon is in good shape but it is still an old car." Max sat in his chair and remarked as he seemed to act like an attorney.

"True. But it is still in very good shape." He paused and gazed directly into Mark's eyes. "What do you think?"

Mark was just then getting a rushed feeling of competition flowing through his veins. "Good shape today but seeing how old it is, and the fact that I need it to last more than a year, I might be willing to buy it for the right price."

Sly smiled. "What would you say if I told you the car was already bought?"

"What! You let me drive it and belonged to someone else!" Mark was angry and not amused.

"Whoa, son, don't get your feathers in a flush! It was bought but as a gift to you!"

"What? Is this some kind of sick joke" Mark said as he looked at Sly.

"No, son. One of our community members, who I cannot name, found out about your plight and donated the money to pay for the wagon." Sly reached inside his pocket and pulled out the key to the car. "The wagon, if you noticed, does not have a print key. They did not have it this model. So take care of the key. I suggest let us make you some copies as backups."

Stunned and in shock Mark replied, "Yes, that would be nice."

Chapter 8: Back to Destiny

Mark was still in shock over getting the car of his dreams and getting it for free as a gift. After the paperwork was completed and Max showed him his way home, Mark just needed some time alone to contemplate what has happened this last few days.

"Do I have some kind of guardian angel watching over me?" Mark pondered as he began to make some coffee. He pulled a mug from the cabinet and waited for his coffee machine. While waiting, he stood looking out the glass doors on the deck at the distant lake. "My life seems to have been a mess. I was lucky to find love thirty years ago but then I wasted it with my job and lost it totally when she died." The coffee machine gave a gentle tweet, a signal it was done. Mark poured his coffee and walked on the deck.

"Now where am I?" He sighed. "I'm in the middle of a beautiful campground surrounded by trees, vegetation, and life and still I am wasting all this worrying about an article on some 150 year old woman I have no idea how to contact without revealing what my purpose is."

He sat on the deck lounge chair just gazing, breathing in the fresh air, and enjoying the moment. This is the first time in a long time he has taken time to just enjoy. The aroma of the fresh brewed coffee filled his lungs as he sipped the warm liquid. He felt release of all the stresses he has endured these past two days.

After finishing his coffee, he laid back upon the lounge chair, closed his eyes and took a deep relaxing breath. Suddenly the image of Anna came floating into his mind. "I wish she was with me today. I wonder what she was doing."

Mark was thinking about her long, blond hair. Her vibrant blue eyes. Her figure. He then gave a laugh. Yes, he may be 50 years old but he was not dead. He then began to wonder how old or young she may be. He did not see any rings on her fingers, no wrinkles, and no idea how old she was. "With my luck, she is young enough to be my daughter or worse my granddaughter and has NO interest in me at all." He thought.

Slowly time past, in which, Mark drifted off to sleep. The sun began to set behind the mountains in the distance and was replaced by the full moon and the stars. The sounds of owls, crickets, and an occasional wolf howl were heard. Lighting bugs with their magical glow dusted the forest making it seem like a fairy tale scene where elves and other magical beasts would come to play. The glow of the moon reflected into the lake which seemed to shimmer and glow with the wind. All mechanical noises were gone. Only nature was heard.

Slowly Mark began to awake. He opened his eyes to all the wonder. "This looks like heaven on earth" he whispered as to not interfere. Taking in all the wonders of the night.

Chapter 9: Finding Anna

The next morning Mark arose to his usual routine. Coffee, breakfast, and then to his computer. He realized he did not get any contact information from Anna so he wanted to try and find her. His excuse? Well, she was said she could help him find a landscaping job. Hopefully she can, but if not, then perhaps he could at least ask to take her for lunch to repay her for her help.

He opened his computer and began to search for the hospital for a phone number. Then he remembered the paper work and rushed to find his wallet where he last stored it. Voila! The paperwork had a phone number. So he retrieved his phone to make the call. He waited anxiously for an answer.

"Hello, Forest General how may I help you?"

"Hello, my name is Mark Anthony and checked out a few days ago after a crash. I person named Anna drove me home but never left her contact information in case I needed her later. By any chance, do you have her number? Or know where I might find her?"

"Let me see...."There was a long pause as typing was heard in the background. "Yes, Anna Baker. Her number is 444-999-0000."

"Thank You!" Mark wrote down the number and her name and quickly added it to his contacts in his phone. Suddenly it hit him. "Anna Baker? Is she related to Louise Baker? What are the odds?" Mark thought as he stared at the number. Then he took a breath and made the call. It seemed like forever before the number rang.

"Hello?" Anna's voice answered.

"Hello, Anna? Is that you? This is Mark Anthony whom you helped drive to my cabin a few days ago. Do you remember me?"

"Yes, I do. Did Max get you a replacement car that you needed?"

"Yes, he did. And, you won't believe it, someone donated money to pay for the car!"

"Wow! How lucky!"

"Yes, I thought so too. But I need to find a job locally and you said you knew of someone who might want to hire a landscaper? I have no real training but I am willing to learn."

Anna laughed, "Yes, I know someone. Brad's Landscaping is always looking for help. They are located not far from where you are. They do work at the campground. It would probably be very convenient for you."

"Great! Can you give me directions or come over and show me where they are?"

"Since you are new to the area, I will come over and show where they are. I will also give you a map of our community so you can know it better. I'm free around noon and will stop by. Is that okay?"

"Yes, perfect! Perhaps I can take you out for lunch?"

There was a slight hesitation, "Okay. But I need to be elsewhere by 1 PM. So lunch needs to be at a fast food."

"Would dinner be better so we aren't rushed? You could bring the map later in the day." Mark felt a bit flushed as he spoke.

"Dinner would be better. I have no duties after 5 PM. So I can stop by between 5-5:30?"

"Perfect! See you then!" They both hung up. Anna felt a bit odd over the dinner but it would be better with her schedule. Mark was dancing around the room and leaping for joy. He was not only looking forward to seeing her but she might be a relative of Louise which would make it easier to find her...at least he hoped so.

Chapter 10: First Date

Mark was primping and eagerly waiting as 5 PM stuck on the clock in the living room. He was busy making sure he had his wallet in his pocket, he ponder over a tie but chose not to wear it. "Too much. She might not see this as a date. For her this is just a get together to pass information." Mark thought as he threw his tie in on his bed. He then fooled with his collar, checked his teeth and impatiently sat on the couch in the living room. He watched as the minutes slowly ticked by forcing himself not to pace and lure around the door peeping out the hole to see her coming.

Knock, Knock. He jumped and ran to the door taking a quick look at the time 5:30 PM. "She's not late." Taking a deep breath to calm himself he opened the door with a grin. "Anna! So glad you made it!"

Anna was smiling and handed Mark the map as promised. "I suggest we take your new car, which looks good by the way, and I will show you where Brads Landscaping is."

"Great! Good plan. "Mark stepped out of door making sure he did not forget the cabin or car keys as well and then locked the door behind him. "Please, after you." He bowed and waved showing her the route to his car.

Anna grinned as she walked to the passenger side of the wagon awaiting Mark to open the doors. A loud beep twice was heard as Mark clinked the button on his set of keys unlocking both doors. "After you," He bowed once more opening the passenger door allowing Anna to enter. He then shut the door behind her and entered the driver's side.

Anna found Mark's bowing amusing and smiled as he entered the car. "Okay, Mark, you need to make a right turn when you leave the campground."

Mark saluted with a grin, "Yes, Mam. Will do." He enjoyed his playing with her. Once reaching the exit of the campground he made the right hand turn. "Now what?"

"We will be making another right turn about one mile from here." As they drove Anna watched for the turn. "There. Turn right there." She pointed to a small road just ahead. Mark once again followed her instructions. "Great. Now we drive about another mile and should see Brad's Landscaping once again on the right." Soon they were parked in the lot in front of the building. A slew of small trees, plants, and other supplies were surrounding the building. It was very obvious it was a nursery who did landscaping.

"Well that was not difficult. Thank Goodness!" Mark said. "I can come back tomorrow to apply for the job."

"Why wait? I can come with you. Introduce you to Brad and recommend you as a starter."

Mark was a bit taken back by the offer. Now he wished he wore his tie. "I don't think I am dressed for an introduction or interview."

"It is a landscaping job. No one dresses up on that job." She giggled. "Plus, my intro will make them more willing to hire you."

"How do you know?" Mark asked.

"I've done it before and they always know I am good with my referrals."

Feeling wary he nodded, shut off the motor and they got out of the car.

"Hay! Brad!" Anna yelled at a man walking among the plants off the side of the building.

Brad turned and saw Anna. "Anna! How have you been?" He walked toward her and Mark.

"Brad, I am fine. I want to introduce you to Mark Anthony." Brad and Mark shook hands. "Brad, Mark just moved in at the campground and is interested in learning and working in landscape. Do you have an opening?"

"Yes, Anna, I do." Then he focused on Mark. "You're not afraid to get your hands dirty are you?"

"No. Not at all. I have always wanted to learn landscaping but spent my time writing and traveling. I think I need to try new things before I get too old."

"Great! Can you start tomorrow? Say 9 AM? I will start by giving you some education and then we will try some landscaping."

"Thank you! I appreciate it!" They shook hands. "See you tomorrow!"

"We have dinner reservations so have to go, Brad but thank you for helping Mark."

"Anything for you sweetheart." And then Brad gave her a kiss on the cheek.

That kiss threw Mark off. "Want now? Are they dating?" He pondered as he entered his vehicle. "So where is this restaurant with reservations?"

"I did not make reservations. Since I thought you wanted to choose where we were to eat. I only said that so Brad would let us leave. He can be a long talker." Anna revealed as they entered his car.

"Okay. Glad you explained. And I have no idea where to eat. Where would you recommend?"

"There is an Italian restaurant in town. Interested?"

"Sounds Good!" So Mark continued to drive to town with directions being given.

Soon, after more directions were given by Anna, they reached the small restaurant, exited the car and entered into a large dining room with a greeter booth at the door.

"Welcome! Anna it has been a while. How have you been? And who is this handsome gentlemen?" the waitress wearing a name tag of "Italy" greeted them as she reached for a menu for each of them and began to lead them to a table.

"Italy, it is good to see you. You look great! I've been fine but busy as usual and this gentleman is Mark Anthony who will be working with Brad's Landscaping tomorrow." Anna gave Mark a wink as she spoke.

"Nice to meet you Italy." Mark was amused with her name but simply smiled and offered his hand. Italy gave him hers and after a quick shake followed her to their table. Mark was happy to help Anna with her chair and then proceeded to sit across from her.

"Would you like some refreshment while you ponder your orders?" Italy asked. They both nodded. "Wine perhaps?"

"Yes, that would be perfect. What would you suggest? Asked Mark.

"The house wine is a sweet red wine with a hint of cherry. Two glasses?"

Anna nodded as she gave Mark a glance looking for his approval. "Sounds delightful" Mark responded.

"So Mark, what interested you in landscaping?" Anna asked. Mark needed to come up with some answer.

"I just never did it before and thought I'd like to try it." Whew! That was close one thought Mark. "What about you Anna? What really is your job? And who do you work for?"

"I work for myself. I am a counselor of sorts. I help people with their issues and help them find resolutions. Kind of like a counselor but no significate genre."

"Give me an example." Mark was curious.

"In your case for example, I was able to help you find a way to get your car, led you to your cabin, helped with keys, and helped you get a job."

Mark was once again taken aback. She sees me as a job! "But I did not pay you for your services, so how is it a job?"

"Bad, example. Sorry." She replied after noticing his response. "For you it started as a job I did as a volunteer, but then I did things for you as a friend." Mark was feeling a bit better but still confused about her job. "I usually called when a business or person needs guidance. Depending of the need I may or may not bill them. It could be helping them with their business management, I bill for that, but maybe just help them with quick problems that they could get from anyone but choose to come to me, more as a friend." Mark still looked complexed. "Less work no money, more work I bill. But I let them know in advance if I plan to bill them."

Mark felt a bit better but still had no idea of what she knew or did. "Are you like a Priest or Shaman who helps but occasionally requests a fee in some way?"

Anna laughed, "I never thought of it that way but in some respects yes."

Italy returned with the wine and they placed their order for some Gnocchi. The rest of the meal was filled with casual conversation and laughs. Mark learned that Anna grew up in Maryland but moved the WV where she could relax more. She loved nature and enjoyed the quiet, calmness of the small town where they were. Anna learned of Mark's travels, his first wife and her death.

"Mark I am so sorry for your loss. I have lost many relatives over the years as well. Now I may have some living but I am not sure who or where they are anymore. I have lost touch."

"Anna, I have heard of Louise Baker. She lives somewhere here or near here. Could you be related to her?"

Anna thought for a second, "No, I am no relation to her. I do know her and where she lives. I am kind a like a friend to her but nothing more."

Mark was trying desperately to not show his eagerness, "Any chance I could meet her? She just sounds like an interesting person."

Suddenly, Anna's mood changed, "So you just want to get to know Louise? I'm sorry, she is off limits. She needs her privacy and I will not invade it."

Mark had just crossed a line. Anna finished her meal in silence and barely spoke to Mark for the rest of the meal. Only very minimal conversation was shared. As they left the restaurant and drove to Mark's house a wide gap had occurred in their relationship. Once at his house Anna did not wait for Mark to open the door but just said "Good Night" and left.

Chapter 11: The Job

Mark awoke the next day feeling angry at himself for messing up things with Anna. "I really did not think that Anna would react the way she did." He thought. Gathering his work clothes he readied himself for the first day on his job. "Thank goodness I got the job BEFORE I screwed up with Anna." Once more he gave himself a quick forced smile while looking in the mirror, a quick comb of this hair, and glance at his wrist watch. "Do not want to be late!" He said as he rushed out the door locking it and ran to his car.

Finding Brad's Landscaping was easy thanks to Anna's help. He soon was parked and entered the main building to search for Brad. The Building was actually a huge barn transformed into a business. Inside off to the right were a selection of flowers, some in vases, and others in fancy pots. On the left were spices and other household plants that could be sold year round as well. The loft looked more like a storage area. In the rear, several stalls away, he could see the office. Walking toward the office, he past the other stalls which contained garden tools, hand and power, and other supplies. The office had a rear wall which was mainly glass and allowed the sun and nature to seen. The front of the office was also formed of glass but had a space in front of it which contained a checkout counter with all the payment needs as well as access to the office.

Brad was seated behind a desk working on a computer as Mark approached and gently knocked on the glass door. Looking up Brad smiled and waved Mark in.

"Glad you made it, Mark. Ready for some training?" Brad smiled, got up and moved to shake Mark's hand.

"Yes, sir! Where do we start?"

"How familiar are you with the garden tools?"

"Some but I probably have more to learn."

With that they walked toward the garden tool section and began the lesson. Mark was handed tools and given detailed explanations of the use of each tools and how to handle them when doing any work. He was surprised at how much he did not know. Learning the technics of how to use them was the most interesting. Then they went to an area on the property where Mark got to practice how to use the tools as Brad left to wait on customers occasionally. The entire day Mark was working at digging, planting, sawing, nailing, watering, transplanting, and later mowing. His job this day was to do things that kept the business working. Brad grew his own plants on the property, which he then sold. Brad also had several greenhouses which were used all year long. At the end of the day, Mark was exhausted but he was very happy as well.

Brad released him to go home around 5 PM. So his work day began at 8 AM and ended at 5 PM. This became Mark's schedule over a month. He was not sent out to do landscaping in the community but had to focus on the businesses gardens and lawns. Mark found that a bit disappointing but he did enjoy the work more than he thought he would.

During this time, he had not seen or heard of Anna. But he really did not seem to have time for her with this job. He was always exhausted at the end of the day and spent most of his time relaxing in the evening. Working with Brad gave him the people time he needed as well.

Then one day, two months later, Brad began to train him on the lawn tractors. That was very new to him. It is then he learned that was the tool which was more complex and mostly used for working in the community. He had to get this right in order to be promoted to the job which might get him on Baker's property.

Brad did his own equipment repairs. Thus he began to teach Mark how to repair things as well. Mark was growing far beyond what he expected when he was hired. Slowly Brad and Mark also were becoming friends.

Then one day in mid-June, as Mark was working on the mechanical repairs of a tracker, he heard a familiar voice from behind.

"Mark Anthony? Is that you?"

He turn to see Anna smiling holding a potted plant. She was beautiful as ever and he loved seeing her grin. Perhaps she had forgiven him?

"Anna!" He said with glee. "I'd shake your hand but I am full of grease and grime. I've missed you. How have you been?"

"I've been well. And look at you! So into mechanics! I am guessing you have learned quite a bit?"

"Yes, I have, actually. I am also finding I love this work as much as my writing."

"Good. Glad to hear it." Anna then got a bit somber. "Mark, I am sorry I reacted the way I did about Louise. It's just that our community gets a lot of people visiting who keep pestering poor Louise. We care about her and respect her privacy so we are very suspect when anyone new asks about her."

Now Mark was feeling guilty for being there to get Louise's story. How could he betray this community, who has been so kind and supportive to him, by doing the interview? He now has a dilemma. But could he explain it to Anna? Not yet, she might over react once again only worse.

"I understand now. I am sorry I asked about her. It's just I was interested in her. I did not mean to offend."

Anna smiled and gently touched Mark's shoulder. "Mark, I realize that now. You have shown these past few months that harming Louise was not your main objective. You have learned new skills and I have heard have done quite well."

"You have been checking up on me?" Mark gave her a gentle nudge with his shoulder.

Blushing, Anna replied, "Yes, I have." She then gazed into Mark's eyes. "When do you get off work?"

"Five o'clock, Why?"

"I thought you could visit me for dinner at my house."

Mark was leaping for joy inside his skin, "I need to clean up first. Also where do you live?"

"I live in the campground as well. At cabin 50. Just follow the signs in the campground. They will lead you there. So let's say 7 PM?"

"Sounds great! See you at 7!"

Anna smiling gave Mark a wave, "See you later!"

Chapter 12: Second Date

As Mark was finishing his work he kept pondering on what was more important. Anna or the story of Louise? All his life he has written but at a cost. He lost his wife and really was not around for her during their marriage. His work had kept them apart, left him no children, and he missed out on so much time with her. But she never complained. He now has regrets that he put his job over time with her. Yes, it offered him a good salary to support her and him—but the loss of companionship must have hurt her as much as it hurt him. But he was young and did not realize what the cost was.

When you are young, the future tends to be all you see. As you age, regrets and loss tend to overcome you. The choices we make during our lives produce the results we see later in them. Chance gives us opportunities but our choices take us down the paths to our destiny. We have some control but are not aware of the results of our choices until it is too late. Or can we change or does chance give us another option?

Mark finished at work and raced home to clean up for his dinner with Anna. He did not want to mess up once again. As he approached his cabin he saw a person covered in a hooded sweatshirt scurry out of his driveway and run down the road. "What's up with that?" thought Mark as he pulled into his driveway. Then he got of his car and made a quick check of the front of the cabin. All was okay but he felt it rather odd that someone would be around his home. Then he quickly rushed into his cabin to get ready.

"No tie." He said as he finished combing his hair and ran out the door. "Now to find cabin 50." As he drove he noticed that the road was sloping downward toward the lake. The trees were fully formed and thick brush was growing below. Then every 300 feet a new cabin was seen either on the right or left side of the road. Once passing cabin 45 he began to slow down so not to miss it. Then it suddenly appeared on his left. The landscape was more level and he noticed her cabin was pretty much along the lake.

He approached the door with a bottle of wine he had grabbed as he left his car and then knocked on the door. As it opened he could see the smiling face of Anna greeting him. "Hello, Mark, glad you could make it!"

"I brought some wine." He said as he entered.

"Great! Follow me to the deck. I am grilling steak and shrimp. There is baked beans and salad on the side."

Mark followed and stepped onto her deck. It was about 200 feet away from the dock where a small motor boat was bouncing with the current. Steps led to the backyard which was connected to dock. The sun was still shining but weakened by the trees and the promise of dusk. Anna had a table set on the deck which was shaded by the late evening shadows.

Anna rushed to grill and removed the steak and shrimp placing them on the table. The salad and baked beans were already waiting. "Dinner is ready!" Anna waved Mark to his spot at the table and both sat to begin their meal.

"This is a really good meal, Anna. Thank you for inviting me."

"It is the least I can do after my actions at the diner."

They each filled their plates. "That steak is really good!" Mark said. "So is the shrimp and …well everything!"

Anna grinned, "So glad you like it." Then after a pause, "So Mark, tell me about your job?"

Mark began to relate how much he enjoyed the work at Brad's Landscaping. He also found that he had a talent for mechanics. Something he did not expect. But he also missed writing and hoped to incorporate his experience in an article sometime in the future.

Anna listened carefully but was not upset with anything he said. Their conversation progressed throughout the meal. As the sun set they remained on the deck with candles lit, drank the wine, and just enjoyed one another's company.

"It getting late, Anna. I have to get up early for work. Thank you for a lovely evening." Mark stood up and Anna walked him to the front door.

"Thank you for coming Mark. I've enjoyed our evening as well." Once they reached the door Mark stopped, turned, and gave Anna a soft kiss on her lips. They both smiled as he walked to his car.

Chapter 13: The Park

The next morning Mark arose humming and singing as he dressed for work. He made and drank his coffee as he nibbled his toast on the deck. The sun was creating a shine on the lake below as the sound of ducks echoed among the hills. Feeling relaxed and happy Mark was enjoying the day as he also remembered his prior evening with Anna. Then glancing at his watch he began to enter his house, lock the deck door, and rush out the front locking it. As he approached his car he neglected to notice the weakness of air in its right front tire.

Reaching his work, he parked his car and proceeded to enter the main building. "Brad! Good morning!" he shouted as he waved to Brad in his office. Brad looked up from his desk and motioned him to come to his office.

"Good morning, Mark. I have some good news for you." Mark was smiling as he anxiously waited to hear more. "My business takes care of Destiny Calls Park Campground. We are the ones cutting your lawn and others as well as taking care of the city park on the lake. I think you are ready to do the lawn and landscape work throughout the campground and the park. The week of July 4th a carnival will be arriving at the park and remain opening during the 4th. We usually have fireworks over the lake. There are picnic areas that need to be well kept. We empty the garbage cans and dump them at the local recycle/garbage dump. I want to take you there today and show you around. The lawn tools will be loaded on the flatbed truck when you do that work. We only take the dump truck once a month to empty the trash. The park has a place for boats to dock and a space is roped and netted off for swimming. We have some lifeguards during the days. No swimming at night."

"I had no idea about the existence of the park in the campground!" Mark said with surprise. "Is it open yet?"

"Yes, it opened Memorial Day a couple of weeks ago. I would have mentioned it but I thought you knew about it."

"I wish I had. I spent that day watching TV." Mark was amazed that he never knew about the activities.

"My truck is over there." Brad said as he motioned to the blue vehicle across the lot. "Let's get in and you can see the park and I can explain the work areas to you."

They got into the truck and Brad drove to the park. They entered from a different road than the one Mark used every day. The trees hung over the road creating a living tunnel of green with glints of sunshine dripping through the branches as the wind waved the leaves. After about a two mile drive with twists and turns that varied with up and downs, they entered an area with a field of cut grass with the road edging along the rim and then ended at the lake where a huge gravel parking lot where some vehicles were parked.

The lake area had a wire fence that protruded into the lake and formed the swimming area. There was a diving board on one end. The lifeguard was sitting on a perch mid-pool with a small shaded roof and a place for drinks or snacks. The area could be closed and locked for safety when no lifeguard was available.

There was also a line of 3 docks where various water vessels could moor. There were about 10 docked thus far. There were some boats pulling water skiers far in lake. Another dock labeled "Fisherman's" was on another space away from the boats and pool area. A lone man was sitting in his portable chair as his fishing line hung over the water.

"Wow! Brad this is beautiful."

"Glad you like it. Now we need to maintain it." Mark listened carefully as Brad explained the care of the grassy field where the carnival will be coming. Then they drove to the area where their picnics ground were hidden among the trees. The picnic grounds were within walking distance of the lake, pool, and docks. But people had to carry their supplies from the parking lot. There was a restroom area located near the picnic grounds. Another one at each dock area and finally one a few feet away from the pool area.

Beyond the picnic area there was another road which led to a small petting zoo with its own parking lot. There was a few grassy areas around that they had to maintain as well as some flowers.

"This park is huge!" Mark said in awe as he gazed about. "I can't believe I did not know about this."

Brad gave a chuckle. "I guess you think you will enjoy doing this?"

"Absolutely!" Mark grinned as he took in the view.

As they left the park, they drove down a road which linked to the one Mark was familiar. They passed Anna's house. "I hear you had dinner with Anna." Brad said.

"Yes, I did. I saw her dock but never knew the park was so close to her home."

"She was lucky to find that home. It was the last one built in the campground." Brad responded.

Finally they passed his house and made their way back to the landscaping lot.

The rest of the day was made up of the normal chores around the business. Brad and Mark discussed the next day's chores they would do together at the park.

As Mark left for home he noticed the tire was very low. He knew the gas/electric station would have the air service he needed so he quickly drove off. Upon reaching the station he went to the air pump, entered his coin and began to add air pressure to all his tires. Then once again he noticed the black hooded person walking past the station and down the road. "Who is that?" he wondered.

Chapter 14: The Park Work

The next day would be the first day at the park. Mark was looking forward to working in the fresh air. He made sure he wore his protective clothing in case of flying debris. As he drove to the Brad's Landscaping barn storage unit located conveniently at the edge of the park, he noticed once again the black hooded person running along the trail inside the park. He wanted to stop and talk to them but they quickly dashed into the wooded area where he could not drive. He has seen that person several times but can't tell if it was male or female due to the hood which was very good at hiding their identity.

Mark pulled into the side road which led to the barn and parked his car far enough away to ensure no interference with the tractor when he drove it out of the barn. He quickly got out of his car, walked to the barn door and used the keys Brad had given him to open the barn doors.

Brad had shown him the barn yesterday and did a good job coaching him on what he was to do that day. Mark had the tractor started and drove it out of the barn. He did have to get off and lock the barn before he drove it further down the road then into the park. Squirrels were dashing up the trees and the birds were screaming as he began to mow the grassy field where the carnival was to come. As he drove he felt the warmth of the morning sun and the breeze from the lake touching his skin. The combination felt like a calm warm bath since the work was also causing him to sweat. He worn an old cowboy hat he found in the barn to help with the glare of the sun. He was glad it had string to hold it on his head as he worked. The breeze could have easily grabbed his hat and tossed it on occasion as he worked.

By noon he had the field mowed but now he had to do the picnic area, the docks, and other spaces so he returned to the barn to retrieve the smaller riding mower for those smaller spaces.

On his way back he saw Anna sitting on a bench outside of the pool area. He glanced at his watch and parked the tractor across from the pool so he could visit. Slowly he snuck up behind her and then spoke, "Anna, fancy meeting you here!" Anna jumped, turned and saw Mark smiling from ear to ear.

"Mark? Mark! What are you doing here?" Anna smiled and laughed as she spoke.

"Well, I am now in charge of the park maintenance. I had no idea this park was here. But I am enjoying my new job."

"I thought you knew about the park. The campground was built around the park which contains the lake."

"Well, sadly, I did not know about it. I, personally, did not rent my cabin. My magazine rented it for me to do my story." Suddenly Mark was ousted by himself and he knew it. The look on his face changed to more solemn.

Anna stood there a bit stunned. "So Mark, you are here on assignment for a magazine."

Mark had a small panic attack and stuttered, "Yes. But I have not written as yet. I am still learning about landscaping."

"Your article will be about landscaping?"

"Yes. I will be writing about my experience." Mark was speaking the truth about his experience but he left out Louise Baker the main topic.

"Okay. Then. I will let you "experience" so you can write." Anna smiled and gave Mark a quick kiss on the cheek and waved as she walked down to the dock where her boat was moored.

Mark felt so bad, so rotten, and yet so thankful that Anna bought his story. He realized he needed to start writing his story soon. He would definitely need to include his landscaping experience.

Chapter 15: Snake in the Grass

As Mark awoke for his landscaping job he also began to realize he needed a plan to meet Louise Baker but it needed to look natural. The Fourth of July was coming in 10 days. The carnival was arriving in 3 days. It would stay until July 5. So he was aware that he needed to put the landscaping job first. He just needed to look for any opportunities that might occur.

The weekend, which was his off time, was approaching. Which means he needs to get the park finished today. "No pressure" Mark sighed as he grabbed his lunch and ran out the door. The carnival area he finished yesterday so things should be fine. Monday the carnival will be setting up and he might be needed to help them. Thankfully that means he will be off work on Sunday July 4th. He wants to definitely spend the day with Anna.

"I wonder if she will be up for a date this weekend? I need to call her!" Once he reached work, he grabbed his phone and called Anna.

The phone rang and went to voice mail. "Anna, this is Mark I wonder if you are free this weekend? Please give me a call to let me know." Mark left his message and began to load the company truck with some tools he thought he might need and then rushed to the park to begin cleaning up the zoo area since he had most of other areas completed yesterday.

He parked his truck in the zoo parking lot, left his truck with a wheelbarrow filled with the tools for working the flower garden as well as some flowers he wanted to add. Upon reaching the flower patch outside the zoo he lowered the wheelbarrow, grabbed his shovel and began to dig some holes for the plants he brought. There were already some perennials growing and flowering but he just want it be a bit more colorful for the Fourth. He chose some red, white and blue varieties that would stand out and enhance the garden. Slowly and carefully he began planting. But during the process he kept hearing a faint noise within the other plants. He chose to ignore it. Just as he finished the last planting he noticed movement as he was bent over just waiting to rise. Then he saw it. A snake. Not just any snake. It was near his head. A brown snake with spots that smelled like cucumbers. It was curled next to him in striking position. Mark suddenly realized it may be a copperhead. They are not known to be aggressive unless they are feeling attacked. They are venomous, sharp nosed pit vipers like rattlesnakes. It was about two feet long. He then remembered they like hiding in brush and mostly eat rats. Now he wished he had vinegar to add to the surrounding garden to deter the snakes. He just never thought about coming across one, especially this close.

Suddenly a group of children were walking toward him. He feared talking since the noise might make the snake strike. The children moved closer, giggling, joking, and then began to yell. He had no choice. "Get away!" he yelled "A copperhead is near my head!" The children screamed, ran into the zoo doors. The snake detonated and struck Mark on his cheek. Mark screamed, arose and ran into the zoo door where he fell to his knees and keeled over. The zoo manager ran to Mark as he instructed the staff to call emergency.

Mark awoke in a hospital bed. His cheek as swollen and red and it was painful. The first thing he saw was Anna beside him. She was holding his hand and her eyes were filling with tears. "Anna" he said.

Anna smiled and wiped the tears from her eyes then held his hand once more. "Mark, you gave us scare!" He then saw Brad was also in the room on the other side of the bed.

"Man I wish I'd given you some warning about the snakes around here. I just never thought about it. Honestly." Brad had a worried look on his face.

"I am okay. Really." He tried to ease their pain as well. "I never thought about a copperhead being in the flower garden! I guess I am an idiot."

Brad smiled, "Friend you're not an idiot. I don't think anyone around here ever expected the copperhead. They usually avoid humans and stick to rats. I, personally, have not seen one in years. What you are is a hero! You put yourself in danger by warning the children visiting the zoo. You will need 2-4 weeks away from work to recover. How long will depend on the severity of the bite."

"But at least I finished the mowing before the carnival comes on Monday." Mark whimpered. "I wanted to help out with carnival set up and as needed."

"You need to rest for a couple of days but if you feel okay by Monday you could still help—just not with physical work." Brad remarked. "Also if the doc okay's it."

Mark smiled and signed with a bit of relief.

Dr. Dye walked into the room. "Hello Mark. I see you had another accident. But this time you were hurt." He was looking at the paperwork from the tests. "Fortunately, the snake did not inject much venom and you got here in less than two hours. That means you should recover, live, and be able to return to physical work in 2 weeks. But we will need to retest you in a week to be sure." He grinned and left the room, "You are a lucky man."

"Lucky? Guess I am." Thought Mark. "I have survived quite a lot recently and now have two good friends Brad and Anna. I, however, want more from Anna."

A nurse entered as Dr. Dye left, "Mark Anthony?"

"Yes." Mark answered.

"You can leave but you will need someone to stay with you until Monday. If you feel okay by then you can be on your own. No physical work for two weeks. You can move around as long as you feel okay. You will have to tend to the bandage on your cheek until it begins to show healing. Then like any bandage you leave it off so you can naturally heal quicker. There might be a slight scar depending on how well you heal."

"He can stay with me." Brad said quickly.

"I can come over, Brad, when you're at work and look after him." Anna smiled. "I can free up my time this weekend. "

"I will be needing you Saturday but I am off Sunday." Brad replied.

Anna responded a bit excited. "Great! On Sunday, if Mark is up to it, you both can come to my house for lunch and a boat ride,"

"Sounds good to me!" Brad grinned and looked at Mark. "Mark is that good for you?"

"Yes! Yes, it is. I am so lucky to have you both for friends." Mark then looked at Anna. She looked happy but a bit disappointed at the same time. Could his use of the word friends hurt her? "I hope not" he thought. "She is more than a friend but I did not feel it was the right time to mention it."

Chapter 16: Healing

Brad escorted Mark out of the hospital toward his truck. "We will stop at your place to get some of your things to tide you over until Monday when you can, if you feel better, go home." Brad opened the passenger door and helped Mark get settled. Mark was feeling a bit weak, sore and out of balance as he entered the truck.

Soon they reached Mark's cabin where, once more, Brad let Mark use him for balance as they made their way to his cabin's front door. Mark opened the door and they entered. "Mark, this is a nice cabin. Do you need help to fill a suitcase?"

"I might need you to lug it out of the closet and to the car."

With that said, they made their way to his bedroom where they completed the task at hand. Mark was glad he kept the place neat and tidy. He would have been embarrassed if he wasn't. Mark chose not to include his computer in the packing. He did not want his story to accidently be seen. He had not written much since he arrived since Louise was not found as yet. He did know he needed to begin it and report to the magazine soon of his progress or rather lack of it.

They left Mark's cabin with the suitcase in the back of the truck and soon arrived at Brad's home.

It turned out that Brad's home was on the other end of Brad's Landscaping just behind the small woods which edged the business. "My home was originally part of a farm. I split it to create my business on one end. Which is why the business is in a barn area." Explained Brad as they parked in the driveway next to the house.

"Let's get you inside first and then I can bring in your luggage." Brad said as he left the car and rounded to the passenger side. Brad was careful as he opened the door and walked Mark to the steps off the front porch. There were only 3 steps but there was a railing which Mark firmly grasped as he moved onto the porch. It was a L shaped porch which covered the front of the house with about a half of porch rounding the right side of the house which eventually had a sloping walkway which could be used for transporting heavy objects onto or off the porch. It was not a steep slope but gradual wide enough as well for a wheel chair. "The side porch was how my father reeled his way with his walker as he got older. We placed a parking spot over there..." he pointed off the side porch, "so my dad could then get into his car. I use that now for lugging in stuff for the house. I don't think I will need to use it for your luggage."

Brad unlocked the house door and waved Mark inside. The main entrance was a hallway where a coat rack, closet, and small table with a phone on it was on one side. The hallway lead to a stairway which lead to the second floor and a doorway of which the door was open and one could see a kitchen. On the other side of the hall was an open area which was the living room and dining room area. Another door to the kitchen was seen on the far end. A fireplace was in the living room section. "Mark, let me take you to the upstairs bedroom I reserved for you and show you the rest of the house."

They slowly walked up the steps where three bedrooms and a bath were located. Brad showed him the one he would be using. "I will run out to the truck and get your luggage. Be back in a minute." Brad rushed down the steps. As he left Mark was admiring the art in the hallway. There were several paintings of nature areas which looked like some spots he saw on the Brad's Landscaping area. Panting but still energetic Brad returned and placed the luggage near the bed. "Do you feel like napping or want to come downstairs and relax or are you hungry?"

"I think I'd like to come downstairs for now and sit on your porch. Do you have to go back to the business or can you join me?" Mark asked.

"I arranged for someone today at the business but tomorrow I will be working and Anna should be here." They both smiled, turned and made their way down the steps to the porch. There was a porch swing where Mark chose to sit and made room for Brad.

"No you prop up your legs and relax there. I will be rocking." Brad said as he waved his hand and then sat in the rocker next to swing. "This is my favorite chair." He grinned as he began to rock back and forth. The air had a light breeze and the sun was shining brightly as they continued to converse. Then about a half hour later a car drove up, parked and out came Italy who was smiling and waving. "I want you meet my darling Italy." Brad arose as Italy reached the porch and they hugged and kissed. "Italy, this is my employee and friend Mark Anthony. Mark this is my girlfriend Italy Bippo. She works at the Bippo Italian Restaurant."

"I do believe we have met at the restaurant. I was there with Anna Baker a couple of months ago." Mark replied as he shook her hand.

"Oh, Yes, I remember. And yes Anna mentioned you were going to work for Brad if I recall." Italy sat in another rocker near Brad's favorite. "I am glad you're working for Brad. He needed more help."

Brad sat back in his chair and reached for Italy's hand as they rocked in unison.

"So you two have been together how long?" asked Mark as he recalled his jealousy the first time he saw Brad kissing Anna on the cheek.

"About 2 years now?" Brad said glancing at Italy for confirmation. Italy nodded as she beamed with happiness.

They continued on with conversation for about an hour when Brad and Italy announced they were going to fix some dinner and left for the kitchen. Mark remained on the porch feeling much better knowing that Brad was not interested romantically in Anna. Now he just had to make a plan for the article while wooing Anna.

Chapter 17: Anna Visits

The next day Mark slowly awoke. The sun was peeking through the drapes which were gently moving with the wind from the window. He heard some mumbling from the lower floor. "That might be Anna!" He yawned and quickly rose to get dressed.

Downstairs Brad and Italy were busy in the kitchen laughing and teasing one another as they sat drinking their coffee. Soon Mark was slowly making his way down the stairs. He wanted to be careful even if he felt he was able to run. Following the laughter he entered the kitchen hoping Anna was there.

"Good morning Mark!" Brad smiled as he sipped his coffee and arose to help Mark if needed.

"No need to help Brad. I think I can manage. I am feeling much better than yesterday."

"Sit here." Brad pulled a chair from the table for Mark who immediately sat down since he felt a dizzy spell. "Coffee?"

"Yes, thank you, Brad." Italy then arose and began to pour Mark's coffee. "So what time do you head off to work?"

Brad laughed. "You seem anxious to get rid me. What I think you really mean is, when is Anna coming."

"Is it THAT obvious?" Mark was a bit stunned but smiling and laughing. "How long have you known?"

"I knew it the first day I met you. The way you looked at her and how you reacted when I kissed her on the cheek."

"So I am that telling?" Mark was now feeling a bit embarrassed but still laughing.

"You kissed her on the cheek?" Italy said with a teasing jealousness. Brad smiled and nodded.

"But she is like a sister. She is not you." Brad touched Italy's hand and looked deep into her eyes.

"I know." Italy said as she returned the gaze.

"Maybe I should leave you too alone!" Mark joked.

They continued their jovial banter as they drank their coffee and Italy made them eggs and toast for breakfast.

The hall grandfather clock struck 8'oclock as Brad left for work. Italy and Mark began the kitchen clean up.

"How long have you known Anna?" Mark asked as he was drying the dishes.

"All my life actually."

"So you grew up together?

"Kind-a. She was there for me whenever I needed her."

Suddenly there was a knock at the door. "I'm here!" Anna yelled as she then entered.

"In here, the kitchen!" Italy yelled placing the last dish for Mark to dry.

"What are you two up to?" Anna said as she arrived at the kitchen door. "Does Brad know about you two?" She laughed looking into Mark's eyes.

"Nothing is going on but cleaning the dishes. No one can replace Brad!" Italy joked. "Glad you made it. I need to get to the restaurant." She then gave Anna a hung and left.

An awkward silence suddenly came as Italy left the house.

Mark looked into Anna's eyes. "So what do you have planned for us today?"

Anna felt a bit flushed. "I thought we would take a walk down to the farm's pond. We could feed the ducks. The walk might help you recover your balance. I see your cheek is not as swollen." She touched his cheek and was checking his bite. It was then she noticed Mark staring into her eyes. Mark slowly and gently kissed her on the lips. Anna pulled away for a moment but then she kissed him back. They gently hugged as they kissed for a very moments.

Mark pulled himself back. "Anna, I really like you a lot." He wanted to say love but felt it might scare her away.

"I like you a lot as well." Anna smiled. "But we do need to get you some exercise so you can go back to work on Monday."

Mark smiled. "We eat dinner at your house tomorrow right?"

"You're thinking of food right now?" Anna laughed.

"No, not really. I thinking of spending time with you."

"Okay. Mark let's go to the pond." Anna quickly moved to the door, then turned and used her index finger to motion Mark forward. "Come on. Grab some bread for the ducks."

They left the house and arm in arm began walking on a path which led to the pond. As they walked the birds were chirping and they heard crickets within the brush. Passing the wheat field, they saw cows grazing in the distance. Soon they arrived at the little pond which several ducks were swimming. There were also some ducks a shore sleeping in the shade of the trees. The wind was moving the water with a gentle push as they watched nature all around them. Anna motioned for Mark to hand her the bag of bread. She then reached in the bag and began to tear the bread into bites for the ducks. They laughed and joked as they threw the bread on the side of the pond.

Mark was feeling the happiest he has felt in years. He felt young again. He was in love and may have found his best life here in the mountains of West Virginia. They walked around the pond viewing the nature and watching the wildlife occasionally show themselves among the grass, trees and brush.

As they fed the ducks and walked the sun moved higher in the sky. "My goodness! We've been having so much fun I forgot about the time. Mark it is noon already! I think we need to go back and have lunch." Mark watched Anna as she motioned him toward the pathway back to the house.

While they were walking along the pathway, they held hands and discussed the pond experience. "Anna, I've got to say it." He stopped suddenly. Pulling Anna near him, he gave her another kiss. When he pull away from the kiss he spoke. "I think I love you, Anna."

Anna was smiling but looked a bit concerned. "I think I love you as well, Mark."

Chapter 18: Back to Anna's House for Dinner

The next morning as the sun peaked through the window Mark awoke feeling more like himself. Actually he felt the best than he has felt in years. He loved his time with Anna at the pond and throughout the rest of the day with Brad and Italy as well. The evening pot roast Anna had made was delicious and he was looking forward to another meal and day with her today.

Mark dressed and made his way to the kitchen where Italy and Brad were conversing over coffee. "Good morning!" he said as he entered the kitchen.

"Good morning to you as well! We plan to be at Anna's at 2 o'clock. Meantime, perhaps, you and I can have a little talk." Brad was smiling and then sipped his coffee.

"Sounds good." Mark enjoyed talking with Brad. More and more he felt closer to him. Much like a brother he never knew.

Italy and Brad continued with their usual bantering and joking including Mark as appropriate. Then Italy shooed Brad and Mark away to have "their" talk.

Brad and Mark moved toward the porch when Brad spoke. "Come with me to the shed over there..." he waved toward a small barn 200 feet across the driveway. "I have something to show you."

Mark followed Brad wondering what it was Brad had to show him. Once they reached the shed, Brad unlocked the door and they entered.

This "shed" was more of a "barn" in size. So why Brad referred to it as a shed he had no idea. Inside was a lathe, a jigsaw and other wood working tools. In another area there was a pottery wheel. And in another spot was an art gallery where paintings were made or in the process.

"This is my personal hobby shed. This is where I spend time creating. I enjoy making pottery, carpentry and carving, and creating pictures in paint."

"I remember seeing some paintings in the upstairs hallway. So they were created by you?"

"Yes. I was rather a youngster of 12 when I did those. But now I am thinking about painting, not just for fun, but to sell." Brad pulled a cloth from the front of a canvas. "What do you think?"

Mark was stunned. The painting was outstanding. So realistic it looked like a photograph. Every detail was seen. It was a painting of a wooded area with every detail of the bark which seemed so real he thought he could feel it if he touched it. There were small animals' semi hidden within the art. Even some insects could be viewed. The leaves were delicate and defined. "Wow! Brad you have so much talent! Yes, yes, your work is good enough to sell. But first I would enter into some art contests and gain some free publicity before you begin selling. Once people see more of your art you will improve your price and sales."

"Thank you, Mark." Brad looked relieved. "But where would I find the art contests?"

"I know some people and will help you get started."

"Really?" Brad was grinned and jumped with joy.

Mark was then shown several more paintings which he loved. He was in awe how much talent Brad had in several areas. A Business owner, artist, mechanic, landscaper and carpenter.

"There is one more thing, Mark." Brad paused and rubbed his hair. "I need your opinion." Mark was curious as to what was coming next. "I plan to ask Italy to marry me during the fireworks on the Fourth of July. Does that sound odd?"

Mark grinned, "No not at all! But will she be able to hear you over the fireworks?" He laughed a little as he gave Brad a tease.

"O my God. I never thought about that. I guess I could ask right before they go off."

"Okay but will you be able to hear her answer?"

"Good point. Any suggestions?"

Mark pondered. "How about asking her earlier. Perhaps on the Ferris Wheel or another ride?"

"Yes, that might work. I really wanted the fireworks though."

"Okay. But ask her at a time when the fireworks are not exploding. There usually is some space between each display."

"Yes, I can do that." Brad nodded. "We need to get to Anna's. She is waiting for us."

So off they went into the house to gather Italy and drive over to Anna's.

Once they reached Anna's, they all were quick to enter and began the social. Anna was once again cooking on the grill and they enjoyed the meal as they joked and ate.

"So we are taking a ride on your boat?" asked Brad. "I have not been on boat yet this year. I've had too much to do."

"Yes, I have it fueled and ready to go." Anna winked as she and Italy cleared the table and went inside the house.

"How are you feeling, Mark?" Brad said as he sipped his coffee. "Feel like a boat ride?"

Mark grinned and nodded as he spoke, "Yes, I am feeling fine and a boat ride sounds nice."

Anna and Italy returned and waved the men to join them as they walked toward the boat. Brad and Mark were quick to rise and follow.

As they reached the boat, Anna and Italy got on first. Anna placed a nautical hat on her head and stepped toward the steering where she began to start the engine. Mark and Brad were busy viewing the lake as they sat near the stern. Italy was talking to Anna once she reached the steering. Soon they were slowly entering the lake. Everyone was smiling and very happy as they followed the lakeside toward the park. They could see the park and several other boats moored at the dock. Other boats were speeding by with some people skiing while holding on to ropes attached to their boats.

"Do any of you ever water ski?" asked Mark.

"I did it a little but I found it a bit scary." Anna said.

"I have done it but not recently." Brad replied.

"I have never tried it." Italy responded. "What about you, Mark?

"ME? No never!"

After an hour of time on the lake they were ready to dock. Anna drove the boat back to her port and slowly parked the boat. "I hope you all had a good time."

They all cheered and thanked her for the meal and boat ride as they left the boat and reached the cabin.

"Well, it is time for us to go. Mark, you have a quick check up tomorrow. If it goes well, then you can begin to help with the carnival. They arrive late Monday and will camp. Tuesday they will need you show them where to connect to the power and just be around to give them information mostly. They usually have their own generators. I will be showing them the property and where they set up on Monday." Brad then patted Mark on the back. "You will be fine."

Italy and Brad left for their car while Mark took a moment to kiss Anna goodnight. "I am feeling much better." He thought.

Chapter 19: Dr. Visit

Monday arrived. Brad took Mark to Dr. Dye for his check up and advised Mark he could go back to work but not any physical work. He had another checkup scheduled for another 12 days later. Mark's cheek was no longer swollen and the bite could barely be seen. He was healing remarkably well.

"Mark I will drive you to your car so you can return home. I suggest you return to work tomorrow. The carnival will be arriving late today and I can take care of it. But tomorrow I will need you at the park early about 7 AM to help them. Remember ONLY help with where and what they can do. DO NOT DO ANY PHYSICAL work!" Brad gave Mark a stern look as he drove to the landscaping lot where Mark's car has been sitting for several days.

Mark nodded, "I understand. No physical work only mental."

Once they reached Brad's Landscaping Mark and Brad loaded Mark's car with his clothes that were used the past weekend and Mark began his drive home to Destiny Calls Campground. As he drove he noticed that black hooded figure crossing the road just ahead. "Who is that?" He thought. "I wonder if I can stop and ask them?" Just then the mysterious figure vanished into the woods.

Once Mark reached his home, he unloaded his clothes and entered his cabin. "Good to be home!" he said as he entered his bedroom and tossed the clothes into his laundry basket. "Now I need to call the publisher and begin to write."

Mark dialed his publisher on his cell phone. After a few rings he answered. "It's about time!" Jules remarked as he answered his cell. "Where are you and how is the article going?"

Mark swallowed hard and began, "Well I am sorry but a lot has happened recently. Besides wrecking my car I have been tending to a copper snake bite I got this past weekend. I just arrived home."

"Wow! Are you okay?"

"Yes, but it has been hard to find anything about Louise Baker. The town is loyal to her and fights to protect her from any reporters or anyone who they feel will harm her."

"Hmm. Sounds like a dilemma. But you have conquered many issues in the past and come up with a good article. I have faith in you. I need the article before Christmas so it is in our January/February magazine. So you still have 6 months. Just call me every 3 months NOT four. I was getting very worried. Especially when you were not returning my calls. I was almost ready to send in someone to find you."

"I am glad you worry about me but please do not send anyone. It will make things more difficult for me to work on my investigation."

"Okay. Keep healthy and look forward to reading it."

"Will do!"

The call ended and Mark knew he had to progressively work to find Louise. Meantime he picked up his laptop, moved to the living room and began to write. He decided to write about the experiences he has had. The article might have to be more about him and the search than about Louise. He chose not to mention the name of the town and to make up names of the people and businesses or just say auto shop, landscaping business, hospital etc. At least that is a start. He knew he would have to rewrite it as he went and how the story would evolve. But it is a least a start.

Chapter 20: The Carnival

Tuesday came and Mark drove and parked his car near the barn at the park. He then climbed the riding mower which was easier to maneuver around the carnival area. He spent most of his day answering questions and watching the carnival set up. The carnival had a Ferris wheel. Several game toss, shooting gallery, and other fun items and a tent for a show. The sun shone brightly throughout the day. The wind was mild but strong enough occasionally to make waves within the lake. The carnival was set up near the lake. He noticed a small stage was added near the pool area but was told the city set that up for the fireworks. They had planned to have a band and some speeches during the Fourth of July.

People were coming and going to pool and docks. He watched the boats and water skiers bounce upon the lake. Many were fishing off the docks as well as the boats as well. Children were playing in the playground and at the Zoo. It was a lot to take in.

"Mark is that you?" a voice was heard from afar. Mark began to look around and then saw Anna in the distance coming from her boat. He waved as she approached.

"Mark you seem to be doing much better." Anna said as she arrived next to him.

"I'd kiss you, Anna but I am on duty." Mark joked as he hugged her. "What are you doing here?"

"I am working with the city to set up the stage for the Fourth. I do this every year. They usually start with a band early in the evening and then before the fireworks they have some speeches and Louise Baker will give some awards to some well-deserved citizens."

Mark heart jumped. "Finally he will actually SEE Louise Baker." He thought. "Anna, will you be giving a speech?" he asked.

"Not exactly. I will be helping Louise during the event now and then." Anna smiled, held her hand over her eyes to shade herself form the sun.

"I had hoped to spend the Fourth with you." Mark replied.

"Yes, we can spend most of the day together. I will only need to help Louise before she speaks and right after."

Mark was drooling at the prospect of meeting Louise. "Any chance of me meeting her?"

"Yes. You might meet her." Anna grinned and turned to see her boat beginning to drift from the dock. "I gotta go! My boat somehow has become unmoored." Anna ran toward her boat before Mark could say anything. He started to rush with her but was stopped by a carnival person who just arrived as Anna left.

"Mark, sorry to bother you but we need you to show us where the electrical connection is near the tent. We have our own generators but may need additional access."

"Sure. Show me what you need." Mark responded. He could see Anna was able to re-moor her boat and was talking to some other boaters.

The rest of the day Mark was helping the carnival make the final set up. They planned to be open to the public starting at noon Wednesday. The Fourth of July was Sunday which would be the last day for the carnival. They would not be leaving until Monday or Tuesday depending on the time it took to pack up. But Mark suspected the take down would be much quicker than the set up.

Later Mark called Anna to see if she when would be free to visit the carnival with him. But due to her prior commitments, she was not free until Fourth. They could spend most of the day together except for the "Louise Time". He was looking forward to Sunday. Meantime he would continue to be around as the go-between for the carnival and the park for the next few days.

Chapter 21: Meeting Louise

Sunday finally arrived with Mark leaping out of bed. He had so much to be excited about today. Anna, experiencing the carnival, the fireworks, and perhaps meeting Louise. He would be meeting Anna around 1PM and they planned to spend time at the carnival. Anna's "Louise time" was around 8:00 PM until the fireworks begin.

During the morning he was busy packing a picnic lunch to share with Anna, Brad, and Italy. Brad and Italy were arriving early to reserve their picnic table near the lake.

Mark had some news for Brad. In the last few days he was able to find and enter Brad's art in some contests. He did ask Brad for permission before he sent in the entries but he told Brad he would let him know once they were accepted.

Finally, just before noon, Mark arrived at the park. He parked near the boats and picnic area. As he left his car, he saw Brad and Italy waving from the distance in the picnic area. Waving back, he lifted his lunch basket and made his way toward them.

"Hello!" Brad said as he rushed to help Mark with the large, heavy basket. "You know you did not have to do this for all of us. We could have brought food as well."

"Yes, I know, but I wanted to repay you for your taking care of me when I got bitten. Besides you did bring the drinks...right?"

"Yes, we did." Italy smiled. "I brought wine, lemonade, and iced tea."

"No soda?" asked Mark.

"I never thought about it. I can go get some." Italy replied.

"No, what you have is fine. I just find it unusual. Most people just grab a soda."

"True. But soda is expensive and not healthy." Brad chimed as he grabbed some chips from a bag Mark brought.

"Well chips are not usually seen as healthy either!" Mark laughed.

"Well according to the bag.." Brad read the ingredients. "Potatoes, oil and salt. Does not sound bad!"

They laughed and bantered while the sat down and enjoyed the view. Soon they saw Anna mooring in the harbor.

It wasn't long until Anna arrived. "Hello Everyone!" Anna cheered as she placed her calendar on the table. "Everything looks good!" She then turned to Mark and gave him a quick kiss on his bite free cheek. Soon they were eating their lunch and enjoying one another's company.

Mid-lunch, Mark decided to make his announcement. "Brad I have some good news for you." He reached into his pocket and handed him a piece of paper. Slowly Brad began to open the folded square. As he silently read its contents he began to grin from ear to ear.

"I have five contests been accepted into for my art! Wow! I need to call and confirm!" Brad wiped a small tear from his eye and gazed at Mark. "Thank you, Mark. I never dreamed this was possible."

Mark returned the smile. "If I have learned nothing else recently, never stop dreaming. Dreams do come true." Then he paused. "But a little effort, which might include choices, might be required."

After the meal they packed their baskets but left them on the table while they chose to visit the carnival. As they walked, they viewed the Ferris wheel, the tents with games and food like cotton candy and caramel corn. Then they chose to take part in the entertainment at the large tent located in the center of the event.

They reached the ticket office. "Four tickets to the show please." Mark requested as he handed them the money.

"You're Mark Anthony, right?" the ticket agent asked.

"Yes." Mark responded not sure why that was important.

"These tickets are free to you. With all the time and help you have given us this week, the boss wanted to thank you with free tickets to the show." He grinned as he handed Mark the tickets.

With a surprised but thankful look he accepted his tickets. "Thank you. I appreciate this. It has been a joy to help."

Soon they were inside the tent and looking for a place to sit. Then a spot which was center stage with a clear view of the ring was roped off and tagged. The tag said "Mark Anthony, Welcome." Mark was shocked. "I have seats saved for me?" Then a clown ran down the aisle and waved him to the seats marked with his name. The clown motioned for him and his group to seat in the area as he opened and removed the rope. "Thank you." He said as he waved Brad and Italy in first and then Anna. He then sat as he spoke to Anna. "I had no idea this was going to happen."

"It is okay, Mark. You must have earned it." Anna replied.

Then tent began to fill with spectators and soon the ring leader entered the spot light and began to introduce the entertainment. They laughed at the clowns, were in awe of the acrobats, lion tamers, dog show, and musicians. The high wire act and others were also captivating. After two hours the show ended and they walked to the Ferris wheel. Mark and Anna entered their seat followed by Brad and Italy in theirs. As the wheel filled they rose one by one until the wheel was full. Holding hands and the bar in front of them Mark and Anna smiled as they circled. Each time they reached the top, Mark would lean over and kiss Anna. Anna was not sure why. He might be afraid of the height and needed to not look or he just wanted a kiss. Regardless of the reason she enjoyed the kiss and ride.

They all got off the wheel, then bought some cotton candy. Continuing on their way, stopping now and then to play games. The sun was beginning to set and it was 8:00 and Anna needed to leave to help Louise prepare for her stage entrance. The fireworks were to begin at 9:30.

"Mark I will return before the fireworks goes off. See you in the front row of the stage area." With that Anna gave Mark another kiss and slowly melted into the crowd of the carnival.

Mark, Brad, and Italy spent another half hour playing games then made their way to the picnic table. They packed up their food and placed it in their cars. "We need to hurry to get a front seat at the stage." Brad said as they walked briskly. Fortunately it was not 9:00 yet. But the seats were getting filled as they arrived.

A band was playing from the rear of stage and a microphone was placed in the center front. There were several chairs on the stage area. Soon the mayor approached the microphone and greeted the crowd. "Welcome to the Fourth of July fireworks!" Cheering was heard from a very boisterous arena. "Tonight we are honoring one of our local residents with our town trophy. Please welcome Louise Baker."

Then it finally happened. From the left side of the stage Louise Baker made herself appear. She was not what Mark expected. Dressed like a nun all in a black robe with a draped veil hiding her face as well as black gloves she began to enter the stage. She seemed to be wearing black tennis shoes and was using a cane as she walked. Slowly she made her way to the microphone. "Welcome everyone!" she said in an old crackled voice. "I have been made aware of a local hero who possibly saved the lives of children at our petting zoo by warning them of the copperhead snake near where they were. He did so at the cost of him getting bitten. He put others above himself. Please Mark Anthony join me on stage."

Mark was astonished. He was totally taken off guard. Rising from his seat he advanced toward the stage. The crowd was cheering as he reached Louise. He finally is meeting her. But not in the way he expected.

"Mr. Anthony please accept our thanks as we honor you." Louise reached behind her and took the trophy from the mayor. "Your heroism is appreciated by our community."

Mark received the award and shook Louise's hand. Then Louise left the stage as the mayor rushed over to shake his hand as well.

"Mark please have a seat." Mark sat in one of the chairs as directed as he watched Louise walk behind the curtain. The mayor said some more things about the carnival, the holiday and the crowd. As he spoke, Mark saw Anna return and sit near Brad and Italy. He wanted Brad to ask Italy to marry him before the fireworks occurred so he tried to get Brad's attention by waving his hand and pointing to his finger. Brad knew what Mark meant but was a bit afraid. Then Mark made a fist and pointed once more at his finger. Brad nodded and turned toward Italy as he spoke. As the town cheered Brad and Italy kissed and a ring was placed on her finger. Anna smiled and wiped a tear congratulating them. Then the mayor spoke. "Mark please come here and press the horn to start the fireworks."

Mark arose and did as asked. As the horn bellowed the fireworks were released from the barge in the lake. He then was given the okay to leave the stage and he ran toward

Anna giving her a huge hug. "You knew about the award didn't you?"

Anna smiled. "Yes, I did."

Chapter 22: Writing the Story

As Mark awoke the next day, he was filled with joy and inspiration. Since he finally met Louise he could begin to write more seriously and "hopefully" get it completed before November. That should give the magazine plenty of time to print the quarterly edition which will be the January/February issue. However, he was not happy about having to leave his Destiny home. He felt more at home in his Destiny than he ever felt any time in his life.

Then he sat at his computer and began to write. He decided to write about his journey to find Louise mostly. The ending is yet to be determined.

Later in the day he left to meet Anna at her house where they were planning a boat ride. He drove into her driveway and parked his vehicle feeling the excitement of seeing her once again. His thoughts flowed. "How could he leave her? How could he leave this place? Could he write from here for the rest of his life? He could write differently. Perhaps more about other things than people and places. He loved to write but he loved his life in Destiny more."

He knocked on the door and was greeted with a warm hug and kiss. "Mark, Italy has asked me to be her maid of honor."

Mark laughed, "Brad chose me for his best man!" He then saw Italy and Brad on the deck. "I guess we are making plans today?"

"Yes! And we still will taking our boat ride." Anna was enthusiastic. Once they reached the deck the conversation was ALL about the wedding. They planned to have it at the park in a large tent where they also could have their reception. Unlike others, they were not willing to wait months to wed. They wanted it to happen on August first.

"We have been waiting for two years. We do not want to wait anymore." Brad said as he grinned and hugged Italy.

"Who will you be inviting?" Mark asked.

"Well, you two for sure!" he joked. "Definitely Louise since she is the one who brought us together. Both of our parents are dead but we do have some cousins and some towns folk."

"You do not need to worry about the guests. That will be our job." Italy smiled as she spoke.

"So what do we do?" Mark asked.

"Mark, you plan a bachelor's party for the eve of the wedding. Anna, you plan the bridal shower." Italy pointed to each as she explained their duties. "And show up for the wedding of course!"

Now Mark needed to plan a party but he wanted Brad to tell to tell him who to invite and what he wanted to do. So soon he found himself in deep conversation with Brad over the details. After all he had less than a month to pull it together.

Anna and Italy were doing their planning as they cooked a meal on the grill. The excitement was very uplifting to Mark. He had never experienced this part of the process. When he got married they eloped. No shower or bachelor party. Then he got his first journalist job and began traveling over the world. He began to realize that his marriage was more of a business relationship than a marriage. They planned a life but never really lived it together.

Now he thought even more about his joy here—with Anna. He loved working with Brad. He loved the park. He loved the citizens here. He loved Anna. He loved them all more than he loved writing. If he had to choose this time, his journalism job would lose.

But now he had to see if Anna felt the same about him. So he had to propose. But he also had to tell her the truth about why he was sent there. That meant possibly losing her. He was not sure if he could handle that.

So during the rest of the day Mark was busy planning how he would slowly tread toward telling Anna the truth about his article. He thought perhaps just trying to get a conversation about the trophy given to him might give him some way to tip toe into the subject. He was not trying to "out" Louise but learn from her.

Then it hit him. An idea. His thoughts bloomed. "It is not about Louise. It is about the lessons and wisdom she has gathered over the years. Her birthday is September 11th. That date in past was when the flu of 1918 erupted. It was a date of major attack on the United States 2001. In 1814 the US fleet defeated a squadron of British Ships in the battle of Lake Champlain, VT. Since 1297 both good and bad things have happened. From the premiere of TV shows: The Carol Burnett, Get Smart, Little house on Prairie, to the war time events. One's birthday is not highlighted by what happened in the past on that day. But by the life that is lived and born. By what choices one makes when events occur by chance. All those choices and events give us wisdom and teachings. That is what Louise is."

Chapter 23: Talk and Plan

The next day Mark was to meet Anna once more to plan their assigned events. Mark was planning to begin the tip toe about Louise.

When he arrived he was quite a bit nervous. Anna notice. "Mark you seem a bit overwhelmed by your assignment. Are you okay?'

"Yes, I'm fine. I was thinking about the trophy I was given by Louise. I wonder if she might have some ideas from her past experiences that might help us with our tasks. I am sure she has a lot of thought of what marriage is and the best way to handle the best man speech for instance."

"She might be able to help but the times have changed since she was young and it might not really be as helpful."

With that remark Mark chose to not pursue it any further at this time.

He was a bit surprised at Anna's ideas for the bachelor's party. After some discussion he chose to keep it a private party at his house. It was going to be more of a cook out with games and watching sports.

Anna asked his help with the bridal shower as well. But he did not have much to add to her plans. The shower would be at her home in a similar fashion only with presents to add to her needs. They were going to keep it simple since Brad and Italy already had ALL the household needs in their homes. They planned to live at Brad's and Italy would be moving out of her apartment.

Anna and Mark both felt perhaps money for them to use toward a honeymoon might be a better idea. They needed to discuss that with the future bride and groom.

The following day at work Mark shared the idea of honeymoon money of which he was very pleased. But apparently they did not plan on a honeymoon until the fall when his business would be less and they could then have enough time to choose a destination.

"Brad you mentioned that Louise brought you and Italy together." Mark asked mid-conversation.

"Yes, she introduced us to one another at an event in park."

"I find her interesting. I bet she has a lot of wisdom that she has shared over the years." Mark was a bit nervous as he talked.

"Yes, I have gone to her for advice off and on over the years. She is usually willing to offer it." Brad gave Mark a questionable look. "Are you needing advise?"

"Actually, yes." Mark took a deep breath. "I want to propose to Anna."

"Great!" Brad smiled and gave him a hung. "When do you plan on doing it?"

"I'm not sure." Mark hesitated. "I am worried that I am too old for her, I have my doubts about asking her and I thought Louise might have some thoughts to help me make that choice...to ask or not to ask."

Then Brad said something he did not believe. "Mark, I can set up a meeting with Louise for you. She would probably be happy to help."

"Really?" Mark said as he was stunned that this might actually happen. If this happens, he plans to tell Louise the entire truth and get her advice on what to do.

"Happy to help!" Brad said as he picked up his cell phone and called Louise. He walked into the other room away from Mark to discuss what was happening with Louise.

Then about ten minutes later Brad returned. "Louise is happy to help. You have a meeting with her at her place at noon. I will give you directions and let you have all the time off you need for your discussion."

"Brad, thank you so much! I just can't thank you enough." Mark was elated and hoped everything would go well.

Chapter 24: Louise

Brad was waiting for Mark at the business when he arrived the next day. As Mark entered the barn, Brad leapt from his office chair. "Mark! Here are the directions to Louise's house" He then handed him a typed piece of paper. "You need to leave at 11:30 to get there on time. You will need to go to the gate and push the enter button. An employee will answer and open the gate. Then proceed down the long driveway and park in front of the house. She lives in a mansion behind the park area."

As the time clicked by, Mark was feeling worried and anxious. "I hope I am doing the right thing." He thought as he continued his normal duties at work. As the clock reached near 11:30, Mark prepared himself. He washed up and changed into a suit combing his hair as usual before he left.

After about 15 minutes of following the directions given to him he saw the gated mansion. On the outside of the tall iron gates was a speaker box about 8 feet off to the left side mounted on an iron post. He pulled up to box and found a button labeled speak which he pushed. A light ring was heard and then a voice. "Welcome. How may I help you?"

"Hello. My name is Mark Anthony and I have an appointment with Louise Baker at noon."

"Welcome Mr. Anthony. I will open the gate then proceed to the parking area in front of the house. I will meet you there."

Slowly the gates began to open. Placing his car in gear, Mark began to slowly drive down the driveway. There were a couple of right turns along the shaded road but he reached the area described quickly. He saw a butler waiting at the mansion entrance.

Mark parked his car, took a deep breath, and exited his car locking it. As he made his way to the butler, he was stunned by the size of the house and the beauty of the landscape. He wondered if Brad was the curator. "Hello. I am Mark Anthony." Mark offered his hand as he greeted him.

"Welcome. Sir." The butler shook his hand and bowed. "Please follow me." Mark followed as requested and entered the main hall. He saw a dining room off to the left and a living room on the right. There was a large coat closet on the side with living room long side a small table with a hat rack, mirror above and a shoe rack below the table. Ahead of him was a door which he had no idea where it went but there was a stairway off to the right side.

He followed the butler up the stairs and into a study or office at the top of stairs further down the long hallway were several doors. He assumed they were bedrooms or at least one rest room. As they entered the study the butler motioned him to the seat in front of a desk. "Please wait here. Ms. Baker will be with you shortly."

Mark waited nervously as he gazed at the bookcases, computer, and other items in the room. Then he heard a shuffle behind him and turned around. Louise was entering the room. She had her normal dark nun like robe, gloves, shoes and her veil covering her face. She walked in slowly with her cane. He stood as she entered. "Good afternoon, Ms. Baker. May I help you?"

"No, I am fine. Please sit." Louise then slowly moved behind the desk and sat. "I understand you are looking for my wisdom about some issues?"

"Yes. I have some dilemma I wish discuss."

"Well, what is it?" She came to the point rather quickly.

"I first need to explain something." Louise just sat there. He could not see her reaction so that made him more nervous. His voice cracked as he began. "I work for a magazine which has assigned me to do a story about you." He then stuttered at bit, "but after living here for several months I have come to realize how much you mean to this community. I respect that you want your privacy. So I have written mostly about my personal experience and growth since I have arrived. But if you could share some of your wisdom for the article I would appreciate it." Silence. That made him even more self-aware. "But you do not have to. I would understand."

The room remained silent. "Second. I have been hiding this article for the most part, especially my main goal given to me, from the community—especially from Anna Baker. Mainly because she is very protective of you and I love her. What I mean is...I did not plan for it to happen but it did. I love her and I am fearful she might not want to marry me for not telling her about my mission and I fear I might be too old for her. She has told me she loves me but hiding this story issue and my age makes me fearful to ask her to marry me. I not only love her, I love this community and the friendships I have found. ALL of those I might lose if I tell her the truth about my mission. I have lived my life all over the world but never really found myself until Destiny. I can't bear the thought of losing what I have found. I want to tell her the truth but I am afraid of the consequences. Any advice you can give will be appreciated."

The room remained silent for what seemed like forever to Mark. "Mark, first of all let us talk about the age issue. What if the issue was reversed? What I mean is what if you were younger than her? How would that effect your feelings for her?"

"There is no way she is older than me. But my feelings would be the same."

"Has she ever discussed any age issue concern?"

"No. But she might be afraid to mention it."

"So, perhaps, you both may be concerned about it but never talked about it." Then Louise paused before she spoke. "Perhaps, you should."

Mark nodded. "Yes, I guess I should."

"Now about your article. I am glad you spoke about it with me. Yes, Anna does protect me." Then Louise arose from her chair. "As long as you only write my wisdom and not my identity, location, and private life, I will agree to share my wisdom. If you write anything about me that I have not approved, I will sue you and your magazine. I have worked very hard to try and live a normal life. I do not like being in the spot light."

Mark was a bit ashamed and felt he was being scolded. Then Louise continued and began to remove her gloves. "But have you ever thought Anna feels the same fear about your difference in age?"

The gloves came off and Mark was viewing rather young looking hands. She then began to remove her robe to reveal a young person dressed in blue jeans and a black hoodie.

"I own Destiny. Your boss rented the cabin through me. I knew you worked for a magazine. I suspected you planned to write about me."

Then she removed the veil. There standing before him was Anna! She had a device around her neck and removed it.

"I was the person who found you after your accident. I called the authorities and after they identified you as my renter, I took you luggage and computer and placed them in your cabin."

Now that the device was removed she now spoke in Anna's voice.

"I do volunteer at the hospital and they called me to help you. I was attracted to you when we met at the hospital but because I was so much older than you I called Max to take you to get your car. Yes, I paid for it. I accepted your dinner invitation and went along with your landscaping job idea. Brad and Italy know who I am. I have known then since they were children. When you began asking about Louise I was frightened and stepped back. Brad kept me up to date on what you were doing. I then thought I might be wrong and you really were doing an article about landscaping. So I returned. I did not expect to fall in love with you. Our age difference worried me. I felt if you knew, I could lose you."

Mark's jaw dropped as he listened.

"Then you got bit by a snake and I knew I had to chance it and keep seeing you. I know you are wondering how I could be looking so young."

Anna took a deep breath and began.

"Well when I turned 100 and did not age, scientists wanted to find out why. I signed an agreement which benefited me financially but they were to not divulge my personal information or I could receive millions more. I wanted a normal life—not the limelight."

Anna was moving about the room as she spoke.

"What they discovered is my cells do not die. Every living thing replicates their cells constantly. The old cells are passed or eaten by the new ones to create a balance. Aging takes place when the ability to replicate the cells begins to wane. We reproduce our cells and create our new body normally every seven years. But my cells never tire of the replication process."

Anna paused to check if Mark was still listening.

"Normal people's cells become tired the longer or more often they are replicated. Mine do not. Our skin reproduces about 30,000 to 40,000 **cells every** minute. That means we shed **a** whole layer of outer **skin every** two to four weeks, or 1,000 bodies worth in **a** lifetime. And underneath your **skin** lies **a** vast network of blood vessels."

She saw the eyes of Mark widen as she spoke.

"At least that what google says. So you see that our bodies change when the replication occurs."

Mark was still in shock but listening.

"I can still get cut, hurt, sick but my immune system remains strong. Normally our immune system gets weaker as we age. But my T cells remain strong so does my immune system. If someone would chop off my head I would die."

Mark was horrified by that possibility, but continued to listen.

"But normal illnesses do not seem to harm me. I have not had a cold in 30 years. When I do get one it lasts a short time and is not severe. They still test me now and then but I am still the same."

Now she had to explain something he might be concerned about as well.

"I can no longer give birth since I had my tubes tied after having my son. He died in the service so I have no grandchildren. The scientists think they might be able to have children in a test tube since they feel my eggs are still being produced. But since I am as old as I am I have hesitated. They want to remove some of my eggs to test my ability to pass whatever gene that has created my agelessness."

Anna stopped moving and made her way to a spot in front of Mark.

"I feared telling you about all this. What I knew, what I have done, and who I am. But I do love you and that means more to me than you can imagine. So I ask you. After knowing all this. Do you still want to marry me?"

Mark was overwhelmed by the revelation that Anna or Louise has shared. But he still did love her. "Anna," Mark arose from his chair taking Anna into his arms. He smiled, "Anna will you marry me?"

Anna spoke, "Yes. I will marry you" then they began to kiss but Anna stopped, "You know, we will need a prenup?"

Mark smiled, "Of course we do" Then they slowly shared a warm kiss.

Our destiny is made by the choices we make when chance appears. Choose wisely.

About the Author

Donna Sako was raised in Wheeling, West Virginia and is currently living in Taneytown, Maryland. She earned her Bachelor of Arts Board of Regents Degree in 1976 from West Liberty State College which is now West Liberty University. Her studies included Social Science Comprehensive, Home Economics and Law. In 2001 she retired from Verizon Communications. She owned and operated Alpha Research, Inc. and served as Executive Director of the Taneytown Chamber of Commerce. During her working career she also served as a Customer Service Representative, Small Business Counselor, Consultant, Teacher, and Competitive Intelligence Specialist.